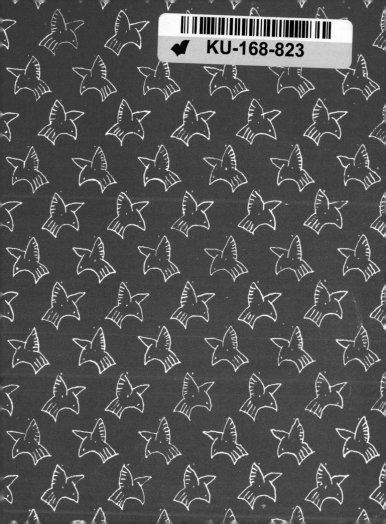

theis Book to Elissa Belogs (handwritten)

Grafton Books
A Division of the Collins Publishing Group
8 Grafton Street, London W1X 3LA

Published by Grafton Books 1986

A TEMPLAR BOOK
Devised and produced by Templar Publishing
Old King's Head Court, Dorking, Surrey RH4 1AR

Illustrations copyright © 1986 by Templar Publishing Ltd
This edition copyright © 1986 by Templar Publishing Ltd

Lear, Edward
The Owl and the Pussycat.—(Edward Lear's
Little Books of Nonsense)
I. Title   II. Crosby, Emma   III. Series
821'.8   PR4879.L2

ISBN 0-246-12867-4

Origination by Positive Colour Ltd, Maldon, Essex
Printed by Tien Wah Press Ltd, Singapore

Edward Lear's

The Owl and the Pussycat

Illustrated by
Emma Crosby

GRAFTON BOOKS
A Division of the Collins Publishing Group

LONDON GLASGOW
TORONTO SYDNEY AUCKLAND

The Owl and the Pussy-Cat
went to sea,
In a beautiful
pea-green boat,

They took some honey,
and plenty of money,
Wrapped up in a
five-pound note.

The Owl looked up to
the stars above,
And sang to a small guitar,

"O lovely Pussy!
O Pussy, my love,
What a beautiful Pussy you are,
You are,
You are,
What a beautiful Pussy you are!"

Pussy said to the Owl,
"You elegant fowl!
How charmingly sweet
you sing!

"O let us be married!
too long have we tarried:
But what shall we do
for a ring?"

They sailed away
for a year and a day,
To the land
where the Bong-tree grows,

And there in a wood
a Piggy-wig stood,
With a ring at the end of his nose,
His nose,
His nose,
With a ring at the end of his nose.

"Dear Pig, are you willing
to sell for one shilling
Your ring?"
Said the Piggy, "I will."

So they took it away,
and were married next day
By the Turkey
who lives on the hill.

They dined on mince,
and slices of quince,
Which they ate
with a runcible spoon;

And hand in hand,
on the edge of the sand,
They danced
by the light of the moon,
The moon,
The moon,
They danced
by the light of the moon.

The End